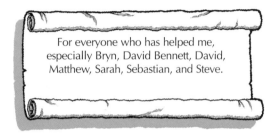

For everyone who has helped me,
especially Bryn, David Bennett, David,
Matthew, Sarah, Sebastian, and Steve.

First U.S. small hardcover edition 2002
The Library of Congress has cataloged the large hardcover second edition as follows:
Handford, Martin.
[Great Waldo Search]
Where's Waldo? : the fantastic journey / Martin Handford. —2nd U.S. ed.
p.   cm.
Summary: The reader tries to follow Waldo as he embarks on a fantastic
journey among the Gobbling Gluttons, the Battling Monks, the Deep-sea Divers,
the Underground Hunters, and the Land of Waldos in search of a special scroll.
ISBN 0-7636-0309-0 (large hardcover)
[1. Voyages and travels—Fiction. 2. Humorous stories. 3. Picture puzzles.] I. Title.
PZ7.H1918Whd   1997
[Fic]—dc21   97-013735
ISBN 0-7636-1922-1 (small hardcover)
4 6 8 10 9 7 5
Printed in China
This book was typeset in Optima.
The illustrations were done in watercolor and water-based ink.
Candlewick Press
2067 Massachusetts Avenue
Cambridge, Massachusetts 02140
visit us at www.candlewick.com

WHERE'S WALDO?
THE FANTASTIC JOURNEY

MARTIN HANDFORD

CANDLEWICK PRESS
CAMBRIDGE, MASSACHUSETTS

THE GOBBLING GLUTTONS

ONCE UPON A TIME, WALDO
EMBARKED UPON A FANTASTIC
JOURNEY. FIRST, AMONG A
THRONG OF GOBBLING GLUTTONS,
HE MET WIZARD WHITEBEARD, WHO
COMMANDED HIM TO FIND A SCROLL AND
THEN TO FIND ANOTHER AT EVERY STAGE OF
HIS JOURNEY. FOR WHEN HE HAD FOUND
12 SCROLLS, HE WOULD UNDERSTAND THE
TRUTH ABOUT HIMSELF.

IN EVERY PICTURE FIND WALDO, WOOF (BUT ALL
YOU CAN SEE IS HIS TAIL), WENDA, WIZARD
WHITEBEARD, ODLAW, AND THE SCROLL. THEN
FIND WALDO'S KEY, WOOF'S BONE (IN THIS SCENE
IT'S THE BONE THAT'S NEAREST TO HIS TAIL),
WENDA'S CAMERA, AND ODLAW'S BINOCULARS.

THERE ARE ALSO 25 WALDO-WATCHERS, EACH OF
WHOM APPEARS ONLY ONCE SOMEWHERE IN
THE FOLLOWING 12 PICTURES. AND ONE MORE
THING! CAN YOU FIND ANOTHER CHARACTER,
NOT SHOWN BELOW, WHO APPEARS ONCE IN
EVERY PICTURE EXCEPT THE LAST?

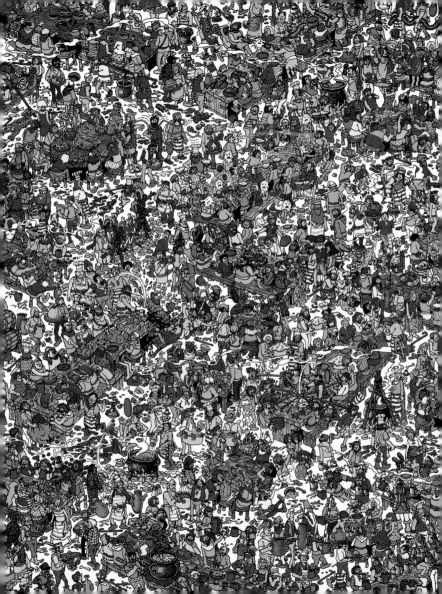

THE BATTLING MONKS

THEN WALDO AND WIZARD WHITEBEARD CAME
TO THE PLACE WHERE THE INVISIBLE MONKS
OF FIRE FOUGHT THE MONKS OF WATER. AND
AS WALDO SEARCHED FOR THE SECOND SCROLL,
HE SAW THAT MANY WALDOS HAD BEEN THIS WAY BEFORE.
AND WHEN HE FOUND THE SCROLL, IT WAS TIME TO
CONTINUE WITH HIS JOURNEY.

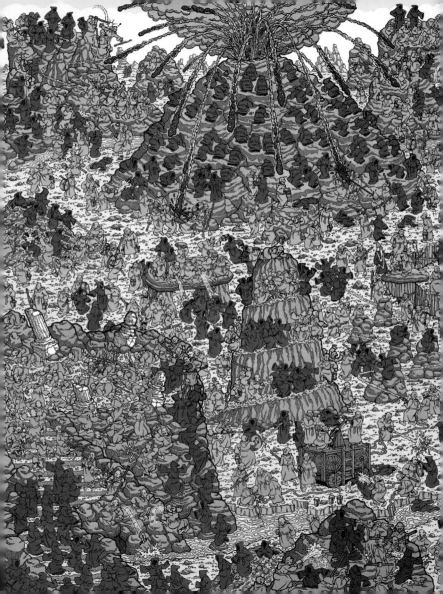

THE CARPET FLYERS

THEN WALDO AND WIZARD WHITEBEARD CAME
TO THE LAND OF THE CARPET FLYERS, WHERE
MANY WALDOS HAD BEEN BEFORE. AND
WALDO SAW THAT THERE WERE MANY
CARPETS IN THE SKY AND MANY RED BIRDS
(HOW MANY, O BRAINY BIRD AND CARPET WATCHERS?)
AND WHEN WALDO FOUND THE THIRD SCROLL, IT WAS
TIME TO CONTINUE WITH HIS JOURNEY.

THE GREAT BALLGAME PLAYERS

THEN WALDO AND WIZARD WHITEBEARD CAME TO
THE PLAYING FIELD OF THE GREAT BALLGAME
PLAYERS, WHERE MANY WALDOS HAD BEEN BEFORE.
AND WALDO SAW THAT FOUR TEAMS WERE PLAYING AGAINST
ONE OTHER (BUT WAS ANYONE WINNING? WHAT WAS THE SCORE?
CAN YOU FIGURE OUT THE RULES?). THEN WALDO FOUND THE
FOURTH SCROLL AND CONTINUED WITH HIS JOURNEY.

THE FEROCIOUS RED DWARFS

THEN WALDO AND WIZARD WHITEBEARD CAME AMONG THE FEROCIOUS RED DWARFS, WHERE MANY WALDOS HAD BEEN BEFORE. AND THE DWARFS WERE ATTACKING THE MANY-COLORED SPEARMEN, CAUSING MIGHTY MAYHEM AND HORRID HAVOC. AND WALDO FOUND THE FIFTH SCROLL AND CONTINUED WITH HIS JOURNEY.

THE NASTY NASTIES

THEN WALDO AND WIZARD WHITEBEARD CAME TO
THE CASTLE OF THE NASTY NASTIES, WHERE
MANY WALDOS HAD BEEN BEFORE. AND
WHEREVER WALDO WALKED, THERE WAS A FEARFUL CLATTERING
OF BONES (WOOF'S BONE IN THIS SCENE IS THE NEAREST TO
HIS TAIL) AND A FOUL SLURPING OF FILTHY FOOD. AND WALDO
FOUND THE SIXTH SCROLL AND CONTINUED WITH HIS JOURNEY.

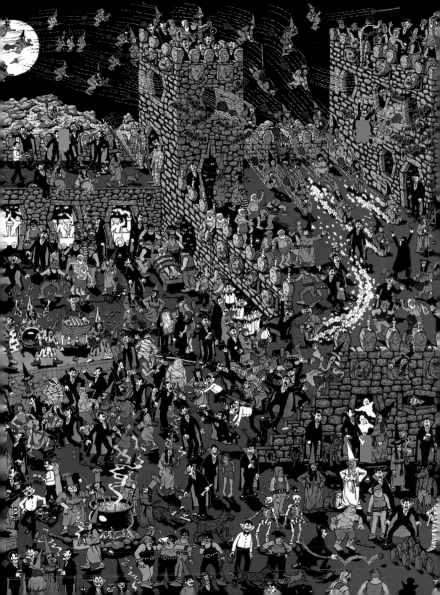

THE FIGHTING FORESTERS

THEN WALDO AND WIZARD WHITEBEARD CAME
AMONG THE FIGHTING FORESTERS, WHERE
MANY WALDOS HAD BEEN BEFORE. AND IN THEIR
BATTLE WITH THE EVIL BLACK KNIGHTS, THE
FOREST WOMEN WERE AIDED BY THE ANIMALS, BY THE LIVING
MUD, EVEN BY THE TREES THEMSELVES. AND WALDO FOUND THE
SEVENTH SCROLL AND CONTINUED WITH HIS JOURNEY.

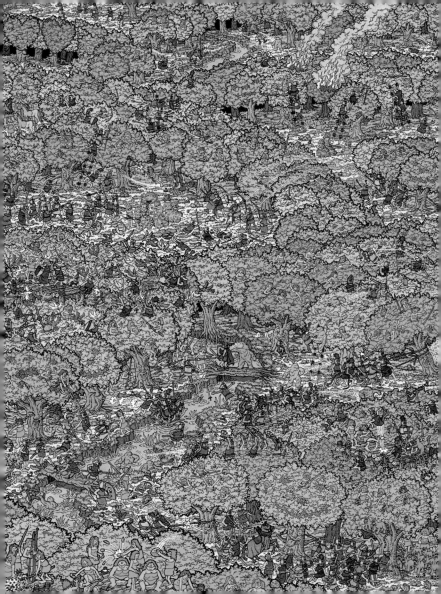

THE DEEP-SEA DIVERS

THEN WALDO AND WIZARD WHITEBEARD CAME TO
THE WATERY WORLD OF THE DEEP-SEA DIVERS,
WHERE MANY WALDOS HAD BEEN BEFORE. AND
WALDO SEARCHED FOR THE EIGHTH SCROLL AMONG
THE MONSTERS OF THE DEEP, AMONG THE MERMAIDS,
FISHERMEN, AND FISH, AND WHEN HE FOUND IT, IT WAS TIME
TO CONTINUE WITH HIS JOURNEY.

THE KNIGHTS OF THE MAGIC FLAG

THEN WALDO AND WIZARD WHITEBEARD CAME
TO A PLACE MORE CROWDED THAN ANY WALDO
HAD SEEN BEFORE, WHERE TWO ARMIES WITH
MANY MAGIC FLAGS WERE LOCKED IN COMBAT.
AND WALDO SAW THAT MANY WALDOS HAD BEEN THIS WAY
BEFORE. AND WHEN HE FOUND THE NINTH SCROLL, IT WAS
TIME TO CONTINUE WITH HIS JOURNEY.

THE UNFRIENDLY GIANTS

THEN WALDO AND WIZARD WHITEBEARD CAME TO
THE LAND OF THE UNFRIENDLY GIANTS, WHERE
MANY WALDOS HAD BEEN BEFORE. AND WALDO
SAW THAT THE GIANTS WERE HORRIDLY
HARASSING THE LITTLE PEOPLE. AND WHEN HE FOUND THE
TENTH SCROLL, IT WAS TIME TO CONTINUE WITH HIS JOURNEY.

THE UNDERGROUND HUNTERS

THEN WALDO AND WIZARD WHITEBEARD CAME
AMONG THE UNDERGROUND HUNTERS, WHERE
MANY WALDOS HAD BEEN BEFORE. THERE
WAS MUCH MENACE IN THIS PLACE, AND A
MULTITUDE OF MALEVOLENT MONSTERS. WALDO
FOUND THE ELEVENTH SCROLL AND CONTINUED
WITH HIS JOURNEY.

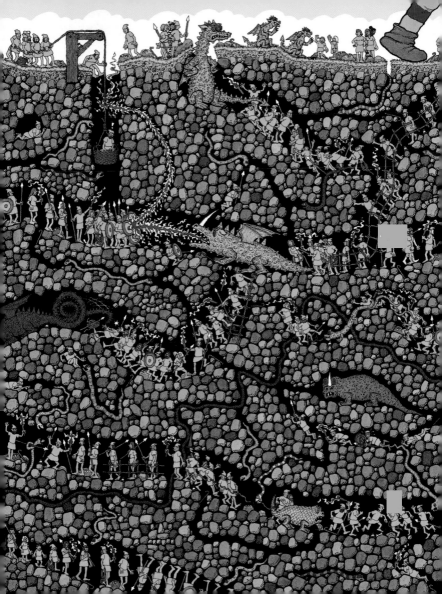

THE LAND OF WALDOS

THEN WALDO FOUND THE TWELFTH SCROLL AND SAW THE TRUTH ABOUT HIMSELF, THAT HE WAS JUST ONE WALDO AMONG MANY. HE SAW, TOO, THAT WALDOS OFTEN LOSE THINGS. FOR HE HIMSELF HAD LOST ONE SHOE. AND AS HE LOOKED FOR HIS SHOE, HE DISCOVERED THAT WIZARD WHITEBEARD WAS NOT HIS ONLY FELLOW TRAVELER. THERE WERE NOW ELEVEN OTHERS—ONE FROM EVERY PLACE HE HAD BEEN TO— WHO HAD JOINED HIM ONE BY ONE ALONG THE WAY. SO NOW (O LOYAL FOLLOWERS OF WALDO!) FIND THE REAL WALDO AND HELP HIM FIND HIS MISSING SHOE. AND THERE, IN THE LAND OF WALDOS, MAY WALDO LIVE HAPPILY EVER AFTER.

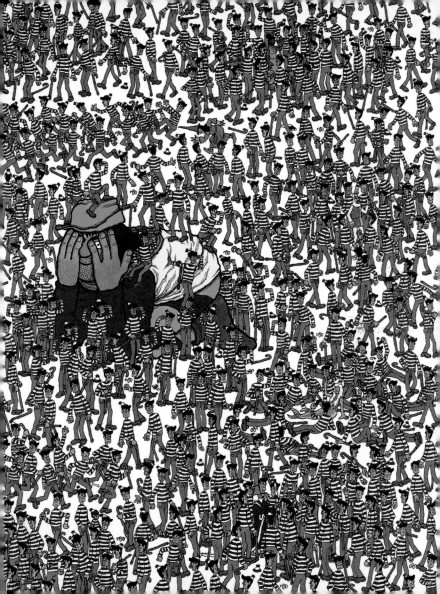

THE GREAT WHERE'S WALDO? 3 CHECKLIST

Hundreds more things for Waldo followers to look for!

THE GOBBLING GLUTTONS

- A strong waiter and a weak one
- Long-distance smells
- Unequal portions of pie
- A man who has had too much to drink
- People who are going the wrong way
- Very tough dishes
- An upside-down dish
- A very hot dinner
- Knights drinking through straws
- A clever drink pourer
- Giant sausages
- A custard fight
- An overloaded seat
- Beard-flavored soup
- Men pulling legs
- A painful spillage
- A poke in the eye
- A man tied up in spaghetti
- A knockout dish
- A man who has eaten too much
- A tall diner eating a tall dish
- An exploding pie
- A giant sausage breaking in half
- A smell traveling through two peole

THE BATTLING MONKS

- Two fire engines
- Hotfooted monks
- A bridge made of monks
- A smart-alecky monk
- A diving monk
- A scared statue
- Fire meeting water
- A snaking jet of water
- Chasers being chased
- A smug statue
- A snaking jet of flame
- A five-way washout
- A burning bridge
- Seven burning backsides
- Monks worshiping the Flowing Bucket of Water
- Monks shielding themselves from lava
- Thirteen trapped and extremely worried monks
- A monk seeing an oncoming jet of flame
- Monks worshiping the Mighty Erupting Volcano
- A very worried monk confronted by two opponents
- A burning hose
- Monks and lava pouring out of a volcano
- A chain of water
- Two monks accidentally attacking their brothers

THE CARPET FLYERS

- Two carpets on collision course
- An overweight flyer
- A pedestrian crossing
- A carpet pile-up
- Three hangers-on
- Flying hitchhikers
- An unsatisfied customer
- A used-carpet salesman
- A topsy-turvy tower
- A spiky crash
- Carpet cops and robbers
- A passing fruit thief
- Upside-down flyers
- A carpet repair shop
- Popular male and female flyers
- A flying tower
- A stair carpet
- Flying highwaymen
- Rich and poor flyers
- A carpet-breakdown rescue service
- Carpets flying on carpet flyers
- A carpet traffic policeman
- A flying carpet without a flyer

THE GREAT BALLGAME PLAYERS

- A three-way drink
- A row of hand-held banners
- A chase that goes around in circles
- A spectator surrounded by three rival supporters
- Players who can't see where they are going
- Two tall players versus short ones
- Seven awful singers
- A face made of balls
- Players who are digging for victory
- A face about to hit a fist
- A shot that breaks the woodwork
- A mob chasing a player backward
- A player chasing a mob
- Players pulling one anothers' hoods
- A flag with a hole in it
- A mob of players all holding balls
- A player heading a ball
- A player tripping over a rock
- A player punching a ball
- A spectator accidentally hitting two others
- A player sticking his tongue out at a mob
- A mouth pulled open by a beard
- A backside shot

THE FEROCIOUS RED DWARFS

- A spear-breaking slingshot
- Two punches causing chain reactions
- Fat and thin spears and spearmen
- A spearman being knocked through a flag
- A collar made out of a shield
- A prison made of spears
- Tangled spears
- A devious disarmer
- Dwarfs disguised as spearmen
- A stickup machine
- A sneaky spear bender
- An ax head causing headaches
- A dwarf who is on the wrong side
- Prankish target practice
- Opponents charging through each other
- A spearman running away from a spear
- A slingshot causing a chain reaction
- A sword cutting through a shield
- A spear hitting a spearman's shield
- A dwarf hiding up a spear
- Spearmen who have jumped out of their clothes
- A spear knocking off a dwarf's helmet

THE NASTY NASTIES

- A vampire who is scared of ghosts
- Two vampire beans
- Vampires drinking through straws
- Gargoyle lovers
- An upside-down torture
- A baseball bat
- Three wolfmen
- A mummy who is coming undone
- A vampire mirror test
- A frightened skeleton
- Dog, cat, and mouse doorways
- Courting cats
- A ghoulish bowling game
- A gargoyle being poked in the eye
- An upside-down gargoyle
- Ghoulish flight controllers
- Three witches flying backwards
- A witch losing her broomstick
- A broomstick flying a witch
- A ticklish torture
- A vampire about to get the chop
- A ghost train
- A vampire who doesn't fit his coffin
- A three-eyed, hooded torturer